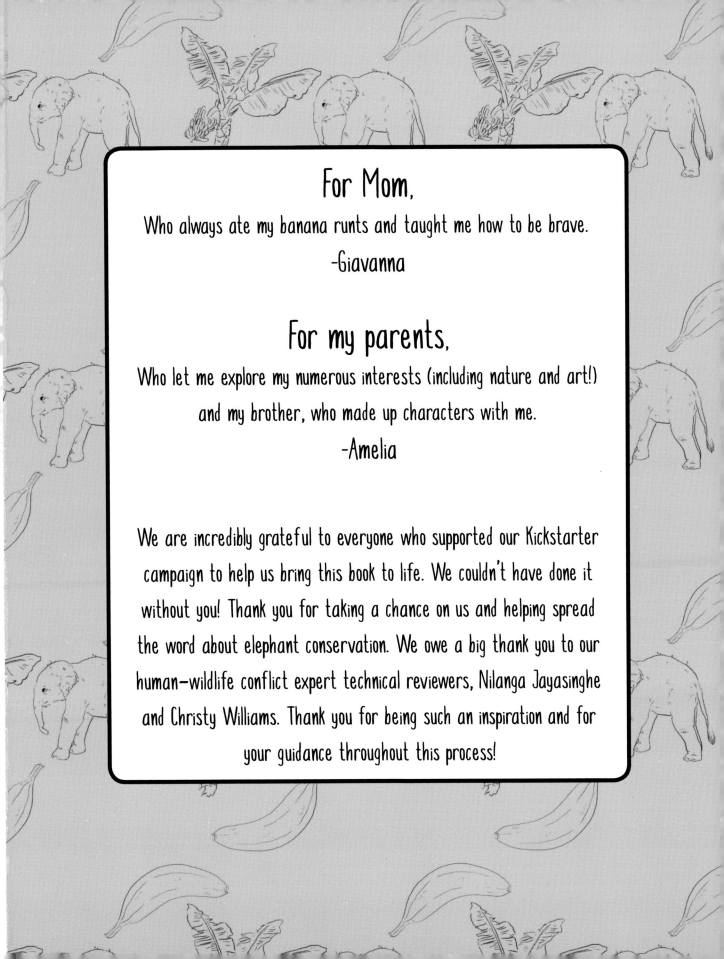

For Mom,

Who always ate my banana runts and taught me how to be brave.

-Giavanna

For my parents,

Who let me explore my numerous interests (including nature and art!) and my brother, who made up characters with me.

-Amelia

We are incredibly grateful to everyone who supported our Kickstarter campaign to help us bring this book to life. We couldn't have done it without you! Thank you for taking a chance on us and helping spread the word about elephant conservation. We owe a big thank you to our human–wildlife conflict expert technical reviewers, Nilanga Jayasinghe and Christy Williams. Thank you for being such an inspiration and for your guidance throughout this process!

www.mascotbooks.com

When Nilly Met Nelly, The Hungry Hungry Ele

©2016 Giavanna Grein. All Rights Reserved. No part of this publication may be reproduced, stored in a retrieval system or transmitted in any form by any means electronic, mechanical, or photocopying, recording or otherwise without the permission of the author.

For more information, please contact:
Mascot Books
560 Herndon Parkway #120
Herndon, VA 20170
info@mascotbooks.com

Library of Congress Control Number: 2016916084

CPSIA Code: PRT1116A
ISBN-13: 978-1-63177-887-2

Printed in the United States

WHEN NILLY MET NELLY,

THE HUNGRY HUNGRY ELE

BY GIAVANNA GREIN

ILLUSTRATED BY AMELIA GRACE GOSSMAN

On a tiny farm in India lived a little girl named Nilly,
Who tended to banana plants in fields just slightly hilly.

Full of pride for her family farm, Nilly guarded every tree,
Helping plant and grow and care for every little seed.

While walking through the fields one day, acting like a forest ranger,

Nilly watched and then she dropped at the sight of potential danger.

A young, fuzzy elephant with peels all 'round her feet

Was feasting on bananas, using her trunk to help her eat.

Nilly heard tales of elephants that roamed
Across fields and forests and sometimes near homes.
But she had never seen one near her family farm,
And feared that this visitor might cause them harm.

So she took a deep breath and stood as tall as she could.
With her hands on her hips, she hoped that she would
Look scary enough to chase her away,
But much to her surprise, the ele wanted to play!

The elephant stomped and she romped and she rolled,
And seemed so much kinder than the stories people told.
"Hello, little Ele. What is your name?
Are my family's bananas the reason you came?"

With the swing of her trunk she said, "My name is Nelly,
And yes, your bananas taste best in my belly.
My family is limited in the food we can find.
You have so many here, I didn't think you would mind!"

"Well," said Nilly, "I suppose just a few,
You're a tiny little ele, how much can you chew?"

The next morning Nilly froze when she made it to the trees,
Because where once stood one ele, **now there were three!**
One of them was giant, at least eight feet tall,
She suddenly felt frightened, and very, very small.

"Meet my sister and Mom," Nelly said while she chewed.
"I told them about your farm and great food.
The bananas are so tasty, I knew they'd want some too,
I thought it'd be okay with a few, plus two?"

"A few was okay though I'm sorry to say,
Your family might eat more than we can give away.
My family sells bananas and that's how we eat,
So you see I must save the bananas on that tree."

"Just a couple more then we'll be on our way,
We'll go find new fields, what do you say?"
Nilly sighed and said, "Well, alright, then.
As long as you promise not to come back again!"

But when Nilly returned to the field the next morning,
She realized she hadn't been firm with her warning.
For standing next to Nelly this time were not two,

But five more eles who had joined their meal group!

Nelly shrugged and said, "I'm sorry but it's true,
We have no other place to go to find food.
There are people farms everywhere and not many trees
Where we're allowed to gather crops for our family to eat."

Nilly felt sad that this story was true,
Though if they ate all her bananas she'd be hungry too.
So she marched to the village and asked all around,
How to keep out the eles, and these answers she found:

"An electric fence, chili,
and honey bees too,

They don't like the noise when
the bees buzz on through."

"Try a trench," said one lady. "They can't get across,
Just dig a big hole too big for them to cross."

So Nilly built a big fence around all the trees,
Then set up some posts for the family of bees,

She sprinkled some chili all over the grass,
And dug a big hole so the eles couldn't pass.

The ele group had now grown to a total of ten,

They stopped for a moment looking puzzled, but then,

One by one, each ele trunk
Tied on tight to the tail of the rump
Of the ele in front and they formed a great line.
Their chain made of eles crossed in no time!

After pushing and pulling across the big trench,
The biggest of them all STOMPED the wire fence!

The eles kept running and the bees buzzed away,
The chili was the last challenge standing in their way.
They scrunched up their trunks and took a deep breath in,
Then sprinted for the bananas, hurray, a win!

Nilly was shocked by the strength of the herd
That foiled her plan as if they'd heard every word.
She had one last option hiding up her sleeve,
One last attempt to make those eles leave.

She needed to find new food for them all,
Though she knew that one field would be much too small.
Elephants are big, and they really like to roam,
So she found several fields for them to call home.

With the help of the villagers she planted new seeds,
For bamboo shoots and tasty fruits to serve as elephant feed.
They made a special trail to help the eles find their way,
Just far enough from the banana fields, but close enough to play.

Now Nilly and Nelly are the best of friends,
And don't need to argue over bananas again.
Everyone in the village has food in their bellies,
Thanks to the humans and their trail for the eles!

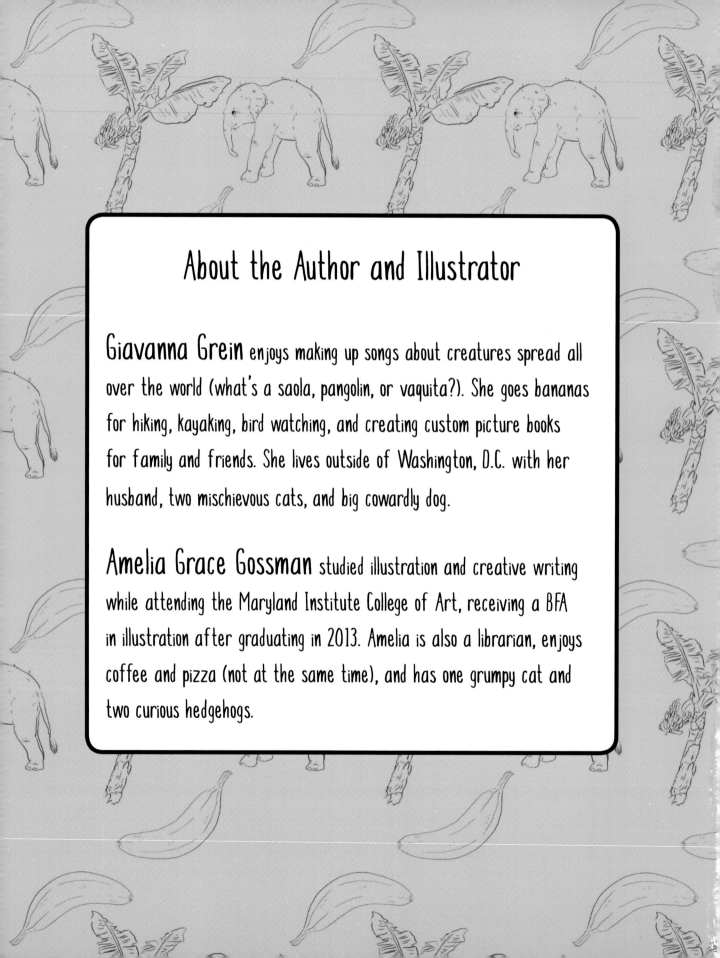

About the Author and Illustrator

Giavanna Grein enjoys making up songs about creatures spread all over the world (what's a saola, pangolin, or vaquita?). She goes bananas for hiking, kayaking, bird watching, and creating custom picture books for family and friends. She lives outside of Washington, D.C. with her husband, two mischievous cats, and big cowardly dog.

Amelia Grace Gossman studied illustration and creative writing while attending the Maryland Institute College of Art, receiving a BFA in illustration after graduating in 2013. Amelia is also a librarian, enjoys coffee and pizza (not at the same time), and has one grumpy cat and two curious hedgehogs.

Want to Learn More
About Human—Wildlife Conflict?

The more we move into wild spaces, the more we run into wildlife. These interactions are often negative. It's important that we learn to live with wildlife because this is their world, too! Each of us has a role to play, from keeping raccoons out of trashcans, to storing human food waste in secure bins to prevent hungry bears from wandering into towns, to finding ways to keep wild elephants from coming into contact with people in Asia.

To learn more about how conservationists are working to prevent and mitigate human—wildlife conflict, check out World Wildlife Fund (www.worldwildlife.org), Human—Wildlife Conflict Collaboration (www.humanwildlifeconflict.org) and Ewaso Lions (http://ewasolions.org/), which are a few of the many organizations working on the issue.

— Nilanga Jayasinghe,
Human-Wildlife Conflict Expert, World Wildlife Fund